The Ketzer

The Ketzer

David Carpenter

HAGIOS PRESS

Copyright © 2003 David Carpenter

All rights reserved. No part of this publication may be reproduced, stored in a retrieval system, or transmitted in any form or by any means, without the prior written permission of the publisher, except in the case of a reviewer, who may quote brief passages in a review to print in a magazine or newspaper, or broadcast on radio or television.

An earlier version of *The Ketzer* appeared in *Descant*, Volume 60; it was winner of the Canadian Novella Contest.

The publishers gratefully acknowledge the support of the Saskatchewan Arts Board in the publication of this book.

National Library of Canada
Cataloguing in Publication Data

Carpenter, David, 1941–
    The ketzer / David Carpenter.

ISBN 0-9682256-7-5

    I. Title.

PS8555.A76158K48 2003   C813'.54   C2003-905080-7

HAGIOS PRESS
Box 33024 Cathedral PO
Regina SK S4T 7X2

For my brother Peter.

Und niemand weiss

Indessen lass mich wandeln
Und wilde Beeren pflücken,
Zu löschen die Liebe zu dir
An deinen Pfaden, o Erd

And no one knows

Meanwhile let me wander
And pluck wild berries
To quench my love of you
Along your paths, O Earth

Friedrich Hölderlin
"*Heimat*," ca. 1805

ONE

1.

Steve Schuyler met Head Kreutzer and his friend in an unusual way. Steve was doing bench presses in the weight room of the Saskatoon YMCA and overheard the following conversation.

"... shoulda bin there, Neville says. Mrs. Potts, she goes out an lops the head off this young rooster, eh? Well, instead of runnin around an bleedin to death, this rooster — an this is no bullshit — *it conserves its energy* an doesn't die. I mean, for days on end it keeps walkin around, I swear to God."

"I'd say you bin reamin out too many toilets lately."

Still on his back, Steve eased the barbells off the stand. He began to count: one, two, three, four. Each press took a four count, two per breath. Each time between rests he would do eight presses. He had worked his way up to one hundred and fifty pounds. One of the guys at the store had told him this was where the bulk was. Steve liked the results but he found the process boring. He switched from counting to words. De–cap–i–tate... de–cap–i–tate.... He tried to think of the word for what happened when you got your balls cut off, but he couldn't remember. It had four beats. It was right on the tip of his tongue.

"Neville told me himself," the young plumber said. "We had this weird conversation."

Still pressing, Steve checked out the two fellows. The plumber was tall, built like a diver or a swimmer, had an abundance of sandy brown hair, a hawk nose, and an amiable twist to his grin. The grin never seemed to disappear. That was Head.

"An get this," Head continued. "Neville says Mrs. Potts has taken to feedin this rooster with a eyedropper down his. . . . "

Puffing now, Steve thought e–soph–a–gus, e–soph–a–gus. He had two more to go, one more to go. At last he eased the barbells onto the stand.

"An this friggin bird is still walkin around."

"Lemme get this straight. Mernie Potts is still feedin this thing?"

"Neville says she uses this eyedropper down his. . . . "

"Esophagus," said Steve.

They both turned Steve's way, one with annoyance, the stockier of the two. He was good-looking, wore his hair long like some hockey players Steve had known, and shot Steve a bumptious look as though Steve had somehow wandered into the wrong dressing room.

The plumber didn't seem to mind. "Yeah," he said to Steve. "She feeds him an he don't know his head's missin type thing."

"Amazing," Steve said.

Head carried on. "I guess they bleed to death, eh, when their heads are chopped off, but Mrs. Potts, she didn't get the jugular or somethin, so this bird he don't know the difference. He flaps his wings, he preens his feathers . . . well, sort of."

The Ketzer

When the two country fellows had left and Steve was back on the bench, he started to wonder about them. They were transplanted, that was obvious. He had the impression that they had more fun than he did, got a bigger kick out of things.

Off came the barbells. Eight more and he could quit. Bench presses. That's where the bulk was. De–cap–i–tate . . . de–cap–i–tate . . . e–vis–cer–ate . . . e–rad–i–cate . . . e–lim–i–nate . . . e . . . e . . . e–mas–cu–late.

Steve was bored with work, where he sold skis and sportswear; bored with weightlifting, which he found even more boring than jogging; bored with Saskatoon, which seemed to have lost some of its appeal since his girlfriend Cora had gotten on as a fitness counsellor for this outfit in Toronto. He was bored with everything, but when he thought about it some, it always came down to Cora's absence. He would probably see her at Christmas, and, knowing Cora, she would re-introduce the subject of marriage, so that thing was in the bag, but in the meantime he was simply wishing time away. He needed some adventure. He needed precisely a three-day adventure, because that's the longest he could get off work before Christmas.

It was September. Steve not only missed Cora, he missed the feeling he'd had each September when they were in university. Perhaps that was it. The old student life was irretrievably lost, the old times gone, the parties not so crazy any more. And Cora, by her phone calls at least, seemed to take this all in stride. She loved her work. She gushed about it.

Steve had liked doing zoo labs, anthropology seminars, travelling with the ski team. He'd liked all those coffee breaks and beer breaks and clandestine parties at his parents' cabin.

That was another thing. When Steve got his job at the Ski Shack, his parents announced the day had finally come when they could move out permanently to BC. Soon after this piece of news, they sold the cabin and that was that. He missed the cabin. He missed the speed boat. He missed the hunting trips out there, or the annual bash he'd throw each fall under the pretense of closing the place down for his parents. Now it was gone. He felt like an orphan. Some of his friends had, like Cora, already left for jobs or schooling elsewhere. Two of them had even gotten married.

Orphaned. At twenty-four.

"I need a new scene," Steve explained to Head Kreutzer in the bar. The beer was starting to work. It was trying to breed enthusiasm. "A new scene," he said again.

The two of them had begun to go for beers on Friday afternoons after work. They chose a large beer hall where Head wouldn't feel self-conscious about his smell. Occasionally it got bad. Head would take off his coveralls, wash his hands and face, and hit the beer parlour by five-thirty. Steve would dress down for the occasion, leaving his tie or sports jacket in the car.

"Huntin?" Head inquired. "Fishin? Booze?"

"Keep going."

"What else is there?"

Steve thought for a moment. The standard reply was sex and drugs. Instead, he said, "There is adventure. Spectacle."

"Come again?"

The Ketzer

He belched. "For example," he said, "there's that chicken at the Potts's place."

"You wanna see that thing?"

"Why not?" said Steve. It was September. A new season, a whole nother ball game, as Head would say.

Head pointed his finger at Steve. "You bring that twenty-gauge of yours and we'll hunt up some grouse along the way."

So they drove halfway across Saskatchewan to an old cabin on the Assiniboine River. Head and his friends often hunted from this cabin. It was hallowed ground, wild on all sides, half encircled by the river valley below.

The Potts's ranch, on the other hand, was a big spread. At the end of the driveway in an aspen grove was a large pre-fab bungalow. Head and Steve were greeted by a pack of mongrels. The two largest dogs came at Steve when he leapt from Head's pickup, and Head had to come over and drive them off.

Neville Potts answered the door. He was a stocky man about fifty-five or sixty with a vigorous look about him. "Yo, Head," he said.

"Yo, Neville."

"How's plumbin?"

"Can't complain. How's the cows?"

"Gettin fatter an meaner."

"See any bucks?"

"Not like there used to be."

Out came Goober, Neville's oldest son. He was tall, balding, looked shy, and had a methodical manner about him. "Yo, Head," he said.

"Yo, Goober."

"Off yer beat some?" said Neville.

"Fartin around," Head replied.

Goober and Neville nodded almost imperceptibly at Steve but there were no introductions. Neville's gaze fell on Head's Toyota pickup. "When you gunna getcher self some proper wheels?"

"Does the job," Head replied.

"So does walkin," said Neville, grinning at Goober.

Head gestured at Steve. "Steve here, he heard about that rooster."

"Head, you didn't come all this way t'see no rooster," said Neville.

Goober said, "Yiz wanna see it?"

Steve said, "Yeah."

Neville and Goober exchanged a look. The four of them went to the henhouse followed by the dogs. The smaller mongrels cowered behind the big ones.

Mernie Potts was there. She welcomed Head and Steve. "You lookin for Flora?" she said to Head.

"No. Is she lookin for me?"

"Don't you wish it," said Mernie. She wore coveralls, a tractor cap, and had a face that was tanned, handsome. Her brown eyes blazed out of her face with a look that could dart either way to anger or delight.

Head looked down at his boots, but as usual his grin never quite disappeared.

"Head, he come in a toy truck," said Goober, laughing.

Mernie led them to a row of square enclosures on the south side of the henhouse, each pen next to a window. On the floor of every pen was a square of feeble sunlight where the chicks stood, squared off, as though in regi-

The Ketzer

ment. A number of mature birds were in the fourth pen. Mernie pointed to an object fastened above the pen. "There's his rack," she said.

His rack? Steve squinted at the object. It was the head of a rooster. Goober had nailed it like a religious object (fetish, Steve remembered later) beneath the archway of the ceiling beams. Mernie plucked it off and stuffed it into Head's jacket pocket. "Add this to your collection," she said.

Neville pointed at something in the shadows beneath the window of the fourth pen. It looked like a dishrag. "There's your miracle bird," he said.

"God," said Steve. He was referring to the smell.

Mernie climbed into the pen and picked it up. The headless rooster had been dead for some time. She said, "I guess he was gettin henpecked." She knelt in the square of sunlight, scattering the chickens, and examined the dead rooster. "Others done him in," she murmured.

Goober said, "Yiz shoulda heard im crow, eh?"

Steve tried to read his face, which was as bland as a dirt road. Was this a friendly smile or a smirk? He assumed the latter: let's show this guy from the city where the bear shat in the buckwheat. "I bet he could talk too, eh?" Steve said.

"No," said Goober, "but he could crow excellent. I'm not shittin ya."

Neville said, "He sort of croaked like."

"Without his head," said Steve.

"Yep," said Goober.

Mernie held the tattered rooster to her coveralls, smoothing down the feathers, kneeling on the straw, and looked down — it seemed tenderly — on the bird. Some roosters nearby began to crow. "He could do lotsa things,"

– 15 –

said Mernie, "but he was none too slick with them hens."

"You'da bin out here when you shoulda," said Neville, "we could of sold im. Or at least we could of et im."

She looked up at her husband. "No tellin what might of happened. You and the boys eat this bird, Neville, his condition might be catchin."

2.

Flora, alias Harry, was the Potts's only daughter. Unlike her brothers, she had made her escape from the farm. She'd only made it as far as Melville, but from there, she and the baby could come back for visits several times a year. A month after Head and that friend of his had visited the family ranch, she and little Carrie came home for the weekend. It was a gritty day in late October. Flora was clearing the table when her younger brother Clyde made a suggestion to the men of the household.

"Head come up for the weekend. He's at the cabin right now. Let's tool over there an get pissed."

Her mother was sitting by the kitchen table changing the baby. Not one to be left out of the action, especially on a visit home, Flora called into the living room where the men sat, "Fine with me."

So all but Mernie Potts, who didn't enjoy drinking, tied one on at Head's hunting cabin.

While her brothers talked hunting at the far end of the table, Flora, getting drunk with unaccustomed speed, began to clamour for her father's attention. He would not even look her way. Then they began to refer to her in the third person and this she never could stand. "Hey, Dad?

The Ketzer

It's my turn now. Dad? You gotta listen, Dad."

She tried her youngest brother. "Clyde! Hey, Clyde!" He looked her way as though a fly were buzzing too close.

"Clyde, it's my turn t'say something. Tell Dad." Clyde gave Flora a blank look and the men talked on. Because of the boozing, their conversation had reached a level where words began to stick together and get replaced by guffaws, yawps, and growls.

"May's well give up, Harry," said the friend from the city. He had soon picked up on Flora's nickname. In fact, he had remembered everybody's name after only one evening's drinking.

"What, Harry give up?" Head mumbled.

"Why do they call her Harry?" asked the new man. Head shrugged.

They were doing it again, talking about her in the third person.

The city man turned at last to Flora. "Why do they call you Harry?" he said.

"Everybody's got a nickname around here," she said. "What's yours?"

"I don't have one," he said. "Maybe I should get one." He turned to his friend. "Why do they call you Head?"

"Because I collect em," Head replied, when the laughter had died down. Head gestured at his trophies, a moose head mounted on one side, a buck's on the other, some hides nailed to two of the walls.

"Collect em or ream em out?" said Clyde.

"I don't see that rooster's head," said the city man.

Head smiled as though he had a private joke. "It's bound to show up somewheres."

Flora looked away. She hadn't joined in on the laughter. "Dad!" she yelled, but Goober just picked up where he had left off. Flora was in this story. It was being told primarily for the benefit of the young man from the city. Flora had heard it so many times, she could mouth some of Goober's words as they were spoken. She wondered if she just cussed a blue streak, could she then get her father's attention. Or maybe, she thought, I might just get the back of his hand.

Goober spoke slowly and methodically. "So me an Clyde here, an th'ol man," he said, nodding to Neville, "we split up. I go up the east side, th'ol man he goes up the west side, Clyde, he's the dog this time, see, because Harry's too tired. He goes real slow through the bush. *Nothin* could get by him. I mean, that bush is never more'n fifty yards wide at the besta times. Well me, I'm waitin, th'ol man's waitin, we hear Clyde barkin like a dog, see?"

The man from the city stopped Goober. "You mean so those bucks will think they're being chased by a dog?"

Clyde turned to him. "You're walkin through a bush surrounded by a buncha bozos with their fingers on the trigger, by Christ you want them to know where you are, an that you don't wear no antlers for a livin."

Goober cut back in. "Anyways, Clyde found the tracks in the snow. He never seen tracks like this one."

"Fresh, you mean?" asked the man from the city.

"Fresh," Neville grunted. "Big!"

"Huge," said Clyde. He formed a heart-like shape with his big hands. "These tracks was the size of a elk, no shit. They was that big, we all seen em."

"I get t'say somethin after you're finished," said Flora.

The Ketzer

"Wait," said Goober. With his tractor cap on, his skinny neck and squawky voice, he sometimes reminded Flora of a cartoon duck. He seemed to be gathering in his memories; this was his story. "So Clyde keeps bustin through the bush, barkin as loud as he can, Head shows up, me an th'ol man we're on point just awaitin. . . ."

Looking at the man from the city, Goober jerked a thumb in Flora's direction, and said, "Here comes Harry outa nowheres, she's got th'ol man's bush gun, an she just stands on the east end of the bush where Clyde come in. She's just standin there, she doesn't wanta be dog no more, she figures it's maybe Head's turn, she's just standin there, I'm ready, th'ol man is ready, an we know — we goddam *know* — there's no way this dinosaur of a buck is gonna get past any one of us. I mean, mister, this is the biggest buck I seen in ten years, rack like a apple tree? Fawwwk, wouldn't you know it, somehow he gets past Clyde — "

"How?" asked the new fellow. "How could he?"

"You tell me," Clyde cut in. "No way in hell that buck coulda gotten by."

Goober resumed his story. "Anyways, there we all are. Out comes ol Appletree — the back way. I yells to Harry, 'Shoot,' I says. Th'ol man he yells out, 'Shoot the bugger!' We're all of us yellin at Harry!"

"What's so new about that?" said Flora.

The man from the city laughed.

"An what does Harry do?" said Goober. He was looking directly at the city man. "What do you think she did?"

The city man gave Flora what amounted to a sympathetic smile. "Shot the buck?" he said.

"Shot the buck, fawwwk." Goober paused for effect. "She

– 19 –

stands there an watches it trot on by. Come any closer, she could of bit off his ear."

"You always tell it wrong," said Flora, her voice sliding downhill. "You an Clyde, you never get it right. Dad, have they ever gotten it right?"

Neville Potts turned at last to his daughter. His broad nose, his cheeks, his massive neck had all reddened throughout the course of the evening. These little beacons on his face were almost the same colour as his old hunting cap. "They got it right, by the Jesus. They got it right. You just stood there with my thirty-thirty like you was usin it for a umber-ella."

"It's my turn now," she said. "I got a question."

"She can shoot a whiskey bottle at seventy-five yards with that ol gun," Neville went on. "Y'think she can hit a buck the size'a Goober's half-ton at ten yards?"

Eventually the laughter died down and Flora asked her question, directed at her father. "Do you think if you was the dog an I was on point I wouldn't some day shoot a buck? Is that what you think?"

Neville looked at his daughter and said nothing.

"A buck, I mean. Not a fawn, not a doe. Just one a them horny ones. D'you think I couldn't pull the trigger?"

Neville looked away. Gone was the anger of the afternoon when the power generator had broken down, the fans had stopped turning, and all the lights in the henhouse had gone out. All she'd done was deliver the bad news and he yelled at her. He wouldn't yell at Clyde that way, not even at Goober that way. As though a brokendown generator were her fault. Or as though by visiting the ranch she had brought them bad luck.

The Ketzer

But the whiskey had mellowed him, it seemed.

"Bullshit," said Flora. "I'd do it. I'd pull the trigger. You don't think I'd some day drop a buck? There's nothin to pullin the trigger."

"I don't know, Honey," said Neville, his voice unaccountably soft.

3.

As he worked a last lump of coal into the cook stove for the night, Steve said, "So, you figure she doesn't go with anyone at all?"

"Got your sights on her?"

"I just wondered."

"She used to see this warden, after her marriage bust up. But the warden, he wasn't what you'd call too popular around here type thing." Head paused as though weighing how much he could reveal and resumed stoking the Franklin at the far end of the cabin. "Way I see it, she works all day at the bank, curls weekends for the women's league, and whatever time's left over, she spends with the kid. She doesn't have no time for no social life. She says she can't *afford* one."

Steve watched the fire in the cook stove. He would need to stoke it and the Franklin one more time during the night. Head was useless at such tasks. Once asleep, Head was always out for the count. "Why do they call her Harry?"

Head dropped an empty forty of vodka into the garbage pail and held up a nearly empty forty of rye, mumbling, "Jesus." He put the second bottle on a shelf near the stove between a bag of all-purpose flour and a box of

Minute Rice. "I think Neville give her that name because he wanted a third son."

"Doesn't he like her much?"

"He *likes* her, as far as that goes," Head replied. "He just doesn't know what to *do* with her type thing. He wants her married again an outa the way."

Steve said, "She should stand up to the old man."

"Tell me about it."

"What happened to the guy she married?"

Head yawned, stretched, and carried the candle to the centre of the room. He began to arrange his sleeping bag on the bunk next to the Franklin. "Mate's okay. He still hunts with me sometimes. Them two just didn't get along."

"Does she ever laugh?"

His friend shook his head. "Serious."

Slowly Steve unrolled his bag, sniffing the mildewed scents of a dozen outings, remembering the feel of every fall when his dad had the cabin and they went hunting. This place was good, too. It would do just fine. He could imagine coming here for years and years. He was down to his long-johns and he wondered if he'd be too warm at first. He turned to Head, by now curled up on the bunk. "You ever . . . you know. . . ?"

"I thought about it a few times," Head replied. "Most guys from around here have looked her over. She's real prime rib, that one."

"But you never actually. . . ?"

"Nah," said Head and blew out the candle.

4.

Neville drove home drunk with Clyde, Goober, and Flora all squeezed together in the cab of the truck. He had driven this road drunk from Head's cabin before. He knew all the trails around here; he owned half of them.

And he still had his temper. Clyde still thought he was God's gift to women. Goober was also unmarried and he still plodded around the barn like an old farmer. And Flora's mum still spent every night alone in front of the television.

"We're all too big for the cab," Flora said.

"You pregnant again?" said Clyde.

"No," she replied, "an I don't have no spare tire like someone else in this cab neither." She gave Clyde an almost affectionate elbow. She felt the full weight of her father on the left and Clyde on the right. Had it been Goober on the immediate right, she would not have felt this constrictive weight on both sides, like being between two steers in a crowded stall. In his shy way, Goober would have leaned into Clyde's body and away from hers. As it was, she had become a sack of feed.

"Think them buggers'll be up at six?"

"Head'll be up."

"They'll be up an rollin."

"Who's the guy from Saskatoon?"

"Buddy a Head's."

"Seems okay."

"They're up for this one."

"Think we should do the top road first?"

"I think we should walk the river valley."

"Couldn't do the river with a hundred dogs an two

hundred guys on point. Too much cover."

"I think we could do the top road first. Some tracks in there. No one's bin up there much."

"I think we should walk the river valley."

"Fawwwk."

"Slow down. There's some tracks in the snow."

Neville slowed the truck, shifting down to second, and just as Flora said, "C'mon, Dad, it's late," a large animal vaulted from the ditch into their headlights, its nose high in the air. It was a white-tail deer, a big buck. Neville slammed on the brakes and the buck squared to face their vehicle.

"Holy Jesus," Neville whispered.

The truck had stalled but Neville made no move to start it up again. The buck stood perfectly still and glared at their headlights. His rack was huge. A tourist could have mistaken him for an elk.

"Appletree," Flora whispered.

"Sure as Christ," said Goober.

The four of them stared at the animal and he returned their gaze with a wavering attention. Then his nose went back into the air as though he were sniffing the stars. As though this truck full of people was, after all, only the second most important thing out there in the snow, and then he launched himself out of the truck's beams, off the road, and up into the woods above the ravine.

"Is Carrie okay?" Flora asked her mother.

Mernie Potts sat in her dressing gown close to the television so that she could hear the program and not disturb the baby's sleep. This was how she had listened to the ra-

The Ketzer

dio at nights when Flora was a child. "I just changed him last ad," she said, without turning to face her daughter.

Flora tiptoed behind her mother and into the room she used to occupy as a girl. She didn't turn on the bedroom lamp. The yard light cast a bluish glow over the baby's crib and Flora bent low over Carrie's head to hear his breathing. He lay on his belly with his head turned away from the light. There was a raspy sound down in the throat from a cough the baby couldn't seem to lose. But he slept. She went silently out to her mother again. A movie was on, an old one. The women wore full-length gowns, crinolines, and petticoats that made them look like flowers turned upside down. The men wore tight-fitting uniforms and swords at their sides.

"Mum, we seen Appletree."

Flora's mother turned slightly. "You smell like a distillery. You smell like them."

"Mum, I'm goin out early with Dad an the boys."

Mernie nodded and turned back to her movie. A love scene was in progress, one of the flowers wilting.

"Carrie'll be fine."

"Thanks, Mum," she said, and tiptoed back to her bedroom. She stood in the glow from the yard light, swaying slightly. Her boy's breathing came regularly between long pauses. That always amazed her, that he could pause so long between each breath. Sometimes she caught herself waiting to see if he'd make it to the next one. She touched his head lightly and his left arm came up to his mouth in a fist.

5.

Neville slept the same way, fist at his mouth, and very slow breaths. He was dreaming about the cattle when the bawling started. But it didn't sound like a cow. It sounded more like a sheep. Why would it sound like a sheep?

Mernie was sitting up in bed. "It's that cough," she said.

"What cough?"

"Carrie," she said. "He coughs himself awake and then he cries." The baby kept crying for a minute or more. It was almost five o'clock.

The alarm would ring in an hour. Mernie put her feet on the floor but just before she could rise, the baby's voice dropped and made a mewling sound to the softer sound of Harry's voice. Neville thought, that's how Harry used to cry when she was a calf. They never sound like people at that age, they sound more like sheep. But it wasn't sheep exactly, it was something else. Neville fell asleep before he could figure what it was. He would be reminded before the day had passed.

6.

Steve held his flashlight up to the snout of a large white-tail buck. Cradled in one of the forks of its rack was a box of wooden matches. As he reached up into the antlers, he felt as though the animal's eyes were real, and at any second he would lower his head and charge.

Shivering, Steve stoked up the stove. The kindling caught at once from the embers, so he dropped in some larger

The Ketzer

chunks of wood and then some coal. The fire crackled. The sound was very satisfying. He took the matches over to Head's end of the big room. It was chilly there, but Head snored away in the warm depths of his bag. Steve opened the door of the old Franklin. A few coals blinked among the ashes, so he started from scratch with newspaper, twigs, and bark from the wood box. Head snored on.

Steve could find no larger chunks of wood, so while the paper and twigs smoked, he went into the storeroom. It was even colder in there than around Head's bunk. A tarpaulin lay over a large pile in the middle of the room. He threw back the tarp and grabbed at what he thought was the dried branch of an old log. It was hard as stone and he let go. The way it clattered with the others on the pile, he knew it was antlers. He held the flashlight on them. There were dozens on the stack, some from spike bucks, but most from bigger animals, enough here to decorate a dozen hunting lodges.

He found the woodpile in the corner and grabbed an armful. As he kicked the door and turned to the Franklin, he heard the paper catch and a *whoosh* from the mouth of the heater. In the orange flare he spotted yet another rack above Head's bunk, that of the bull moose. He looked as though he had just arrived and stuck his head through the wall. He seemed somehow opposed to the presence of these men with their guns and their liquor. A look of stupefied disapproval hung on his long lips.

Head snored on.

Steve stoked up the old Franklin and waited till there was a good roar before he returned to bed. He looked back and forth at the buck, the moose, and then at a lynx hide nailed to the near wall. He thought about the big stack of antlers in the anteroom and wondered how these men could have even the slightest doubt of success this weekend. The woods were seething with life. It was just a question of finding a bunch of fresh tracks, setting up a drive and picking off the best bucks to come out of the bush.

He checked his watch. It was a little past four in the morning. He had to get some sleep, so he tried to think of one object that would hold his attention so that his thoughts would stop flying around the room. He settled at last on Flora.

TWO

1.

Growing up small among bigger kids and older brothers, Flora learned to look up at the world. Sometimes her long brown hair got in the way so she would toss it back and look up sideways just to see the faces of those she walked with. This adjustment would produce a look of elfin bemusement, so all sorts of people would call her cute.

She was quiet. She learned secrets. If you were small and quiet there was security in whispered secrets. And of course power in being thought cute. Her nose and chin were fine and pointed, almost witch-like, her eyes a mossy hazel. One assumed she held many more secrets than she did and that various enchantments lay behind her smallest gestures.

She played a game that was a secret from everyone but her mother. She would pretend she was invisible. When the feeling came over her, she would shrink from sight behind a curtain, a bale of straw or a bush, and watch. If someone spotted her, brothers being the usual offenders, the perfect feeling would be destroyed. But if she remained undiscovered for as long as she wanted to be invisible, the game was fine.

Humans didn't always co-operate, but animals did. She would sit perfectly still in one of her spots (usually a large copse with a pond dubbed Flora's bush in the middle of the lower meadows) and the deer would feed around her unperturbed. Sometimes they would graze the alfalfa within a few yards of her hiding place. On some occasions they seemed to know she was there, but also seemed willing to *pretend* she was invisible. Once she touched a moose calf on the haunch while the cow across the pond looked off in the other direction. More than once she was surrounded by a brood of ruffed grouse chicks while the hen pecked away at the swath on the edge of the copse. She had memories, too (which she didn't trust), of talking to bears.

When Flora began to fill out and lose her desire for solitude, and stopped being a tomboy, and (in his typically contrary way) her father started calling her Harry, the disappearing game was forgotten. At nineteen she married Maitland O'Donnell, a man's man who was like a brother to Flora's brothers, a lazy handsome popular boy who failed at almost everything and came to feel tremendously sorry for himself. He and Flora began to fight, he took to drink and bullying, and in the summer when he left to find work on the oil rigs, she had an affair.

She told her mother her marriage was on the rocks. She even told her a censored version of the affair, how it had ended, how the man in question was now in Europe.

"Men want to be like them bucks," was Mernie Potts's response. "Off with the other bucks an no women please, we got better things to do. Except in rut, an then look out. They get their noses in the air an next thing you know, you're all they ever wanted."

"Well, there's some truth to that, I suppose," she said, putting her hand on her belly.

"Oh, my God," said Mernie.

The Ketzer

Oh, my God, said Flora a year later to herself as she remembered this conversation. She remembered it with some bitterness, because there was so much she couldn't tell her mother, so much more she couldn't tell Neville and the boys or Head Kreutzer or the guy from the city. And Goober, who always meant well, how could he have known what was really going through her head the day they ran into old Appletree? How could he know, for instance, that she was pregnant? That she'd been fraternizing with the enemy, so to speak.

"Oh, my God," Mernie had said, and when she said it, Flora clammed up.

That's when the men had come in for lunch. They'd been trying without success to get a buck. There seemed to be fewer legal deer each season, a fact Goober always left out of his Flora vs. Appletree story. They were all in a bad mood. Neville blamed the road construction crews, the grain farmers, the wardens, and the government. There were fewer places for the deer to hide and soon they'd all be driven down into the river valley, most of which would soon become a federal sanctuary with no hunting allowed.

Neville said to Flora, "Harry, you know that river valley. Them lower meadows, eh?"

Flora looked away.

"Why not come along this afternoon? You can have my bush gun."

"I dunno," she said.

"Do you good," he said. "Besides, you know every one of them bucks by name."

Clyde asked her where Mate was.

"Where he always is. Gettin pissed with his friends."

David Carpenter

"Never mind Maitland," Neville said. "Harry, you find us old Appletree an we'll all get pissed like one big happy family." He smiled at Goober and Clyde. He knew his daughter and her friends in the bush. Last year she'd spent more of her holiday time down by the river than she had on the ranch.

"I bet you'd rather be a buck than a rancher," she said to Neville, Mernie's theory about men still playing over in her mind.

"Be a bit lonely," he said. "Them other bucks, they know what I'm like. They wouldn't trust me."

Neville had begun using a new Winchester with a scope. He figured it would change his luck. He hadn't brought down a white-tail in several years. He handed Flora his old bush gun and seven shells and offered to show her how to stuff them in, but she gave him an impatient look which meant, do not underestimate me, so they all shuffled off to Goober's half-ton, Head in the box, and made their way in silence toward the lower meadows. She took them there, a fact Goober always forgot when he told the story. Sure enough, the tracks were everywhere; among them, a half-dozen does and one big buck.

"You an Head be the dogs for the first bit, hey?" said Neville, and Flora went off into the bush, she and Head barking and howling back and forth till she was hoarse and exhausted. Head went forward and managed to put up some does, but the men on point held their fire. They moved up through the hills of the narrow meadow, Flora dragging behind, thinking about her last fight with Maitland. (He had accused her of making him feel like two cents in front of her friends from the bank. She had countered that all he cared about was fixing his goddam snowmobiles for hunting and she wouldn't mind him looking like a grease monkey half the time if at least he got paid for it.)

And then the part that Goober liked to tell: As she topped a big rise where the meadow narrowed and then widened, the river down to her right, the wooded hills rising to the ranchland on her left, still replaying her fight with Maitland, she came to a stop. Something was wrong. The big copse in the centre of the meadow, surrounded now by the men, was hers. Flora's bush. Head was ambling up to it as though this bush wasn't special in any way. And down toward the river and its thick fringe of bush and trees, rose the knoll she had dubbed Gopher Mountain. With the recent sifting of snow it reminded her of the head of a bald man. She'd given the knoll its name on a hot afternoon scarcely two months earlier — something seemed to move in her belly.

"I am the Ketzer," she whispered.

She walked on in Head's tracks and prayed there would be no buck in the centre. When she reached the edge of her bush the only sound was Clyde's barking and she thought her prayer had been answered. She slumped away from the wind and wished she were back at her apartment in Melville, lying on the couch where the sun came in, with a cup of hot chocolate, and her mum in the easy chair, just relaxing, gossiping, planning what they would eat for supper. Then she realized she was holding a loaded rifle on her shoulder. A desolate little laugh shook out of her chest.

And there was Appletree. One second he hadn't been there; the next, he was out of the bush walking toward her.

Clyde's voice boomed out of the woods: "Hey, you guys,

there's some big tracks in here!" Goober was looking her way, several hundred yards up the meadow, and Head doing the same on the other side of the bush. They were all yelling at her, even Neville, whom still she could not see: "Shoooot the sonofabitch!"

The huge buck walked her way, head low, as though he had just played a trick on someone and was trying to sneak past. She wondered if she'd known him as a fawn. He looked directly at her. She wished she could be invisible again. And then, for a few seconds, she was invisible, and she knew it, because old Appletree was looking right through her, or pretending to look through her. "Yes," he would say if he could, "I know you brought these turkeys out here, but I will forgive you and play along with this old game of yours."

As he passed by she smelled the warmth of him.

The men began to run toward her, their voices getting louder and angrier. His tail went up like a rabbit popping from a burrow, his head came up, and he bounded into the woods toward the river. A few seconds and she couldn't even hear his progress through the trees.

Goober was more aghast than angry. "What in the name of Jesus," he cried.

Thank you, God, she whispered.

She and Goober exchanged a quick brother and sister look.

She would never be able to tell Goober her side of it, because he would never listen long enough. She would likely never be able to tell the guy from the city either. Steve. That was his name.

2.

"You got a hangover?" Steve asked Flora, handing her an extra pair of gloves he discovered in his pocket. Ordinarily he would have said, do you have a hangover.

She put on the gloves and said, "You mean you don't?"

"Nope," he said, "I never go to bed after drinking without taking an aspirin and a glass of water. Never fails me."

She stood on the trail with her hands in the pockets of her parka and clamped her limbs to her body, shivering, staring at nothing. Her dad's old thirty-thirty leaned against a fencepost.

"You know what Head has in the storeroom?" he said.

"No."

"A stack of antlers this high," he said, exaggerating slightly.

"Wouldn't surprise me," she said, and shivered.

"Where does he get all those antlers?"

"He gets some from Dad an the boys. He gets some from his friends. He shoots the rest himself. Mostly after huntin season's over."

"What's he going to do with all those antlers?"

"He's your friend."

He didn't want to sound as though he were quizzing her, so Steve waited for a moment. "My friend the poacher."

"Your friend the trophy head dealer," she said. "A real good rack'll sell for five, ten thousand in the States."

"Is it legal?" he asked.

"About as legal as poaching."

He gave her a grin. "You seem to know a lot about this racket."

She executed a bleak little dance, shivering out loud, her arms at her sides, turning and bobbing in a small circle like a puppet, and all the features of her face, the fine pointed nose and chin, the hazel eyes, the pursed lips holding back (it seemed) on dozens of things to be unimpressed with, endeared themselves to him. Perfectly. He wanted to ask if she ever considered laughing once in a while. Instead, he said, "How much would you get for Appletree's rack?"

"About a year's suspended an a three-thousand-dollar fine."

Steve laughed but Flora looked grave. "Guys keep killin the trophy deer, the whole breed suffers. The gene pool, it gets. . . ."

"Impoverished?" he offered, and wondered where she would learn such words.

She looked at him. "Yeah."

"So what are we doing out here?" Steve asked, holding his rifle out in front of him.

"I go out now an then, hunt with Dad an the boys. But *legal*. I'm not makin war with bucks an I'm not makin money."

"Sounds okay by me," he said. After a while he asked, "You ever get to Saskatoon?"

"Not since I had the kid," she said.

"Just wondering."

"I better stand at the other side of the bush," she said, yawned, and stumped off slowly up the trail that cut through the woods.

"You might want that," he said, pointing to her father's gun.

"Oh," she said, "I might just."

3.

The snow began to fall around noon. They put up a doe and a fawn that morning, but saw no sign of a buck. For lunch, they went off to Head's cabin and had some stew. Flora told Neville that maybe she should pack up Carrie and head for Melville.

"Not if you want some wild meat for the winter," Neville said.

"Magpie or gopher?" she said.

"Just never you mind," said Neville. He almost grinned at Flora and she almost grinned back. So she stayed.

THREE

1.

In the last year of Flora's marriage, but before her pregnancy, her husband Mate went to Alberta to look for work on the rigs, and Flora took her two weeks off from the bank and went home at haying time. It was hot. She spent her time down by the river picking berries.

One day Head went by, trolling from his motorboat. She spotted him first and hailed him from the shore. He wore a bathing suit and a striped towel over his head that looked vaguely Egyptian.

"Catch anything?"

"Na."

He was hunched over in the stern, squinting at her. The sun had reddened him all over.

"Excellent hat y'got there," she said.

"What's in the pails?" he asked.

"Saskatoons."

"Bit late for saskatoons."

"Yep."

"You gettin any competition down here?" he said.

"Haven't seen any yet."

"They're around," he warned. "I'd bring a rifle if I was you."

"Well, you ain't," she said.

The Ketzer

He'd always had a thing about bears. As Head and Flora talked, she caught him giving the bush a circumspect look with his watchful grey eyes.

"I hear you bin plumbin in the city."

"Yeah," he said, disconsolate.

They sat on the clover by the riverbank. It was like being in high school again, one of those days for playing hooky and talking about what you'd do as soon as you left this dump behind. One of those days when anything had seemed possible.

"That's good," she said finally. "You guys earn good money."

"Tell me about it," he muttered.

When he could find no tracks, he seemed to forget about bears, so he helped her pick the saskatoons. He towered above most of the bushes and got quickly to the best berries, eating about a third of his take. After a silence, he said, "Know what? We're like frickin doctors. No one wants nothin to do with us till there's a major disaster type thing, then it's 'Oh, Mr. Kreutzer, we thought you'd never show up.'"

Flora said, "I read where you guys get the same as teachers an cops."

Head didn't seem to hear. "You come home on the bus, people look at you like you got the clap. You tell people what you do an they have this way of lookin at you. Like you was dirt?"

"I'm sorry I asked," said Flora. Her day was beginning to sag.

"You're dirt," he went on, "until their sewer lines are blocked, an zappo, you're a goddam saviour. You know what I have t'do sometimes t'get ridda the stink?"

"Look," she said, "I'm not your social worker. Besides,

you're not the only one with troubles, okay?"

He looked at her then in a way more personal than resentful, and she always wondered what he saw, with the bushes between them and something dawning on his hawk-nosed reddened face, his perpetual grin faltering for the first time ever, because from then on, from time to time, he seemed to look at her differently. She told him about Maitland, the temper tantrums, the long brooding sessions, the drinking bouts and blackouts, and that silenced him.

Then the grin returned. He said he might be back the next day, if it were nice, and went down to his motorboat. As it chugged into the slow current and disappeared around the first bend, Flora was left with the impression of his almost perpetually grinning face. Their conversation came back to her and she began to enjoy it. It was the only complete conversation she'd had with him in years, just him and her, with no brothers to interrupt, no father to drag him away with man talk. And that personal look he'd given her when she'd told Head her own troubles — as if in the vacancy of this place by the river, a true friendship could begin, love could begin, her whole life could begin again . . . because for the first time he was seeing her as —

Not a noise exactly, more like a presence on the path behind her. The edge of a smell. Rotten, musky.

She turned slowly. It was a scruffy male, black except for the beige nose, down on all fours, watching, moving his head myopically from side to side, sniffing her, as though Head had conjured him for her out of his own fears and left him there.

The river lay fifty yards to her right, and the path up the hill to the grazing land was blocked by the bear. At her

The Ketzer

back were the saskatoon bushes, impenetrable to her, irresistible to the bear. At her feet were two pails half full of saskatoons. The idea, she saw, was to get over to the riverbank and all that open space, and to let the bear into the saskatoons, but not into *her* saskatoons. He seemed to wait proprietorially, as if to remind her that it was, after all, his land she was on.

She began to wish for invisibility, and when that didn't work, she talked to the bear. Not words exactly, but an old language of crooning syllables, slow rises and falls in a voice that seemed to come back to her from somewhere.

The bear stopped moving his head.

Later she would wonder where this monologue had come from, the bear words or whatever they were, but at the time, bending to pick up her pails, and moving slowly to her right, and crooning in her woodsy Esperanto, she did not wonder in the slightest.

The bear watched as she backed towards the river.

"Per-heps you could put the berries on the ground," someone said behind her.

She stiffened. The bear bolted and crashed through the trees out of earshot.

Beside a beached canoe stood a man, smiling. He was very tall and thin, his skin and hair so fair, his teeth so large and white he seemed to have been bleached like linen in the sun. She had never seen a man so blond, a face so homely in quite that way: the bulging teeth, the shy delight, the cotton whiteness of his skin, the frolic in his eyes. And he was clapping. It was a formal clap, his long fingers faintly, nervously tapping the palm of his left hand reminding her of words she never used, like virtuoso, concerto.

"That was wary good," he said.

She stared at the man in search of a category: clown? giant child? albino? All those strange words (*lederhosen*?) had nowhere to go.

"What were you saying to him?" the man asked.

"Who are you?"

He told her his name.

"I am the warden's assistant," he added. "The bears are my clients."

He wore the regulation shirt and badge, the government logo was on the prow of his canoe, the rifle stowed beneath the seat beside a battered guitar. She tried to recall his name. Not a syllable would come.

"Were you anxious?" he said.

For a moment, perhaps, Head's stupid prowling fear had become her own. "No," she said.

He laughed nervously, like a fool.

"What did you say your name was?"

Again he told her. It sounded like someone spitting out food. She'd never heard the guys talk about this one. He had to be new.

"Would you do me the extreme plesher of having tea with me?"

She squinted up at him and shrugged.

"Your name?"

"Flora."

"Flora!" he whispered, as though she had given him a password. He laughed again, a nervous gasping knee slapping whinny of a laugh accompanied by much shaking of the head. "Anyway," he said, hunkering down with his thermos in one hand, some cookies in a small bag in the

The Ketzer

other, "you are amazing, your name is amazing, your friend the bear is amazing, the day is. . . . I have had an amazing day," he said, his face at last restored to normal, gentle and pious and absolutely serious.

She asked him where he was from.

"I am chust three months over from Germany," he said and smiled. "I have studied for a while at Heidelberg, my father has a small chalet in the *Schwartzwald*, my hair is blond, my eyes are blue, I am good at science, I love to climb and hike in Bawaria. I am the perfect German cliché. They should make me into a sign and hang me on a hotel in the Rhine for all the tourists to behold." Again the nervous chuckle, the gasping for air.

He offered her a cookie and a mug of tea and she offered him some berries.

"You moved to Canada so's you could get to be a *warden*? Did I get that right?"

"Not exactly. This chob is my research. I am exchange student in environmental studies. I am doing total immersion in all things Canadian, then I write my see-zus. I want to go beck with a Canadian accent. I want to blow them away. I'm learning Country and Vestern. I'm telling you, Flora, Canada is a fantastic place."

"Write a see-zus?" she said.

"Ya. A long research paper," he said, and leaned back on his elbows in the sand.

She got the impression that if a bird were to call, he would worship it; if a fish were to break the surface, he would worship that, too; and if she spoke anything at all, he would worship her voice and immortalize her words in song. That was their first day together; she would remember it from all the others as the day they met the bear. That night she dreamed she met the warden's assistant in the dark by the river and he glowed like a light bulb.

2.

On the second day she woke up early and took a walk even before Neville and the boys were up. She watched the stars fade and the sky light up clear as the wind blew warm across the ranchland. The sky was ripe with . . . what? Premonition, was that it? Either she would meet the bear or she would continue her conversation with Head, or neither would happen, or something else momentous would. Another warden's assistant, this time from Mexico.

After breakfast she went down with her pails to the same spot on the river. At mid-morning a boat came around the bend in the river, the warden's assistant. "Flora," he called out, before his canoe had reached shore, "do you have office down here?" and laughed his nervous laugh. He wore an old shirt and cut-offs. It was his day off, he announced. This time he helped her with the picking, treating each ripe cluster like a string of pearls, and in two hours they had filled both pails. At last, when the heat and the mosquitoes began to get to them, they went over to the river, she in her bathing suit, he in his cut-offs, and waded into the cool boggy water.

"Do you think we could do this in half the rivers of Europe, ya? Only now do we begin to clean them up."

She admitted she'd never been there.

"This country. Fantastic. In my see-zus I try to discover why Canadians seem to hate it so much."

3.

He returned on the third afternoon, once more on a day off, and brought some food in a cooler for both of them. "Some nice patriotic Canadian cheese and sausage," he said. They sat and munched by the riverside. "No more wisits from your landlord?" he said.

"No more wisits," she said.

"Here's to the landlord. *Zum Wohl der Herr*," he said.

"What did you mean by people here hating their country?"

"Name chust one thing about this place you love. One thing."

She thought a moment. "Bears are okay. This valley. All the plants, Mum's apple trees — no, they dried up an died. . . . Deer, I like those. Grouse. Nice fresh air."

"It's all disappearing. The family farm. Good farm land, topsoil, mallards. Not so many bucks this year, hm?"

"There's lots of everything around here."

"No more grouse habitat to the north? No more grouses to the north. Spray with some kinds chemicals, no more hatches. No more marshes up on the flatland, ducks can't nest. Shoot all the big bucks, fewer deer, smaller deer. I tell you, Flora, everything you love you kiss goodbye like your mama's apple trees."

Now he was sounding like some kind of government man. "That's horseshit."

"This is what they said to people like me when there were lots of buffalo, lots of vooping cranes, hm? Ever hear of the pinnated grouse?"

"Should I?"

"No. It's gone. Forgotten. Anything that nurtures, anything that grows up to be beautiful, it becomes a target. Around here, if it runs on four feet, hop into the ski-doo and bang bang cowboy. The natural flora? Poison it. The topsoil? Grind it down wiz tractors, plough it up and vatch it blow away, ya? Vatch it pile up in the ditches."

"How do you get off preachin sermons to people who live here? A foreigner, for God's sake. I suppose things are just rosy over there, are they?"

"No, no. The land is in a great death agony all over Europe. This I know. I have seen the figures." He turned to her, looking dolefully around him. "I am worse than foreigner. I am an alien from a dying planet. That's how I see myself. I have come down to Earth to send a warning."

4.

On the fourth day it rained on and off throughout the morning, so she waited until noon to go down to the river. He was waiting for her, this time back in uniform. He was looking grave. He said he could only stay for his lunch break. They shared a mug of his tea and some date squares she'd brought along and ruminated beneath the big poplars by the river bank.

"It's a fantastic country," he told her, breaking a long silence. "Utterly fantastic. But when I warble like this to the guys around here, the young guys, they say things like, 'I can't wait to go to somewhere else.' The farmers with moneys, hm? They tear their living out of the soil and for what? To go to Texas in vinter and spend it all. I tell you, Flora, they hate this place like a prison cell."

"But there's people like that everywhere."

The Ketzer

"People everywhere don't live in Paradise. They chust live in the world. They live in apartment blocks and malls and refugee camps and ghettos and places where the seasons have no meaning. Where day and night.... I am depressing myself. I am being a bummer, ya?"

"Ya," she said.

5.

Another rain came and went in the night and the morning was sunny. Mernie spotted her daughter from the main barn, in her bathing suit, heading for the lower meadows with her pails.

"Flora, we got more saskatoons in the kitchen than we ever had. You wanta help, you c'mon in here."

"Can't get a tan in the barn," she sang out. "I'm on holidays, remember?"

Beside the path through the woods down to the lower meadows a small creek gurgled with fresh rainwater. Everywhere the dripping trees seemed to exhale humidity. The wind down on the meadows was laden with timothy, sweetgrass, clover and all the re-opened life of the valley.

She was sure the warden's assistant would show up.

He brought two bottles of wine in his cooler. They drank wine, ate berries, and went wading again in the shallows.

"I'll never leave here," she said. "I got no ambitions to fly south."

"You're special," he said. "You talk to the bears. When I go beck to Germany, I will write my see-zus and do propaganda speeches for the Green Party. But you will talk to the bears.... What are you looking at?"

"You."

"You look in a funny way."

"I was just thinkin," she said, "if I took away your ideas, what would be left?"

"More ideas."

"But after all the ideas, after the last idea, then what? This wine must be gettin to me. Am I makin sense? Who are you when you're not makin speeches?"

"The rest of me is a travesty. I am," he smiled, "without a personal life. I am a head full of facts and eloquence and a few good jokes." His nervous laugh sputtered like an apology.

"You never been married, never wanted to have a family?"

"Once in a while I have a . . . pash? A crush, you call it? My biggest crush was for my astronomy teacher *im Gymnasium*. What about you?"

She told him about her marriage, at first haltingly, a veteran who rarely speaks of battle. She felt bolder as the story went on. She even told a fuller version than the one she had given to Head Kreutzer.

"Well, your boosing creep of a husband is a fool, ya?"

"Yup."

"You should wait for a tall blond alien with flashing white teeth and forget about these *Höhlenbewohner*, hm?"

"Purple teeth," she said, laughing.

"Und zo are yours."

The whitey blond hair, the way his skin went from fair to brown from day to day, the nervous explosions of apologetic laughter, the bulging purple teeth, the eyes as blue as a lake, those last words, *Und zo are yours*, the berry taste of his mouth: these things burned into her dreams and lived

The Ketzer

there as though at last they had found a place on the earth to reassemble and call home.

She nicknamed him Whitey.

At the end of the fifth afternoon, a little wobbly and serene, Whitey went back up the river intoning libations. "Gott bless Flora. Gott bless Canadian wine. Gott bless the creatures . . . the creatures. Gott bless the creatures!"

Their lovemaking was done on blankets in the shade of some huge gnarled poplars in the last of the hot afternoons. It was a place close to the river so they could cool off. They soon became reckless and went everywhere naked through the woods together. To escape the mosquitoes they would climb the rounded dry knoll well above the swampy river bottom country but well below the ranchlands, not far from Flora's youthful hiding place among the lower meadows. They christened this knoll Gopher Mountain. On a dare she would stand on the knoll and stretch her body for all to see, but no one saw. She showed her secret hiding place to the young man and he looked on it with such reverence he seemed to be contemplating an ancient graveyard. She tried to persuade him to enter the copse but he wouldn't. He said the brambles were too thick.

They had a week of afternoons in all without so much as a suspicious look from her mother. And years later, whenever Flora smelled the peculiar blend of poplar leaves, timothy, and clover, or smelled ripe saskatoons, she would remember how the breeze would greet her body like the breath of God, divide against her face, and tremble behind her like the joining riffles of a creek.

6.

On the sixth afternoon they were lying naked on Gopher Mountain looking down on the forest and the river below. Suddenly Whitey jumped to his feet and yelled out into the valley, "Eros! Eros! Eros!" He blocked out the sun as he stood above her. He looked like a tree or a cairn.

"Lost your dog?" she said.

"Something I *always* want to do," he said, chuckling away.

"What were you yelling?"

"I must explain," he said. "Once upon a time, in the high mountains of Soana, there was a young student seeking after truth. If you're a German you have to find truth up in the mountains. And this young guy, he climbs away up to a willage. The people in the willage tell him stay away from der Ketzer, this old man up in the alpine meadow. He's crazy. But he's a young man in search of truth so he finds the old guy up there."

"What's a ketzer?"

"I can't think of the word in English. . . . Heretic? Ya. Anyway, it's a beautiful day, chust like this. Out on the meadow the . . . how do you say *die Ziegen* . . . the goats are chumping around and making little goats, and there is der Ketzer, looking himself wary much like a goat. You almost expect he makes his love with the animals and the grass and the flowers, hm? And I forget what happens. I think maybe he tells the young student what truth is, but what I remember is even better. The old goat of a man, he stands on this knoll and he sees the birds and the bees and he yells out, 'Eros!' He sees the goats going at it, ya? And he yells out 'Eros!' And he looks around him — if I were the young student I

— 50 —

The Ketzer

think I would have fled — and yells out, 'Eros!'"

He looked at Flora, somewhere adrift between his pious and his gleeful state, and said, "Always I want to be der Ketzer chust once."

"Well, you answered my question," she said.

"I did?"

"If I strip away all your ideas, what I got left is a horny old goat."

"That's good," he said, and went silent. "You know, the whole problem with man is with the head."

"This is more ideas, right?"

"Only one more learned discourse and I promise you my lips are closed. Eros is the life force, ya? It is the enemy of — what? — thought, consciousness, science, of *Logos*. Eros is opposed to all those things we can think up to make us secure from the capriciousness of Nature. Houses, lights, the . . . uh . . . das *Gesetz* . . . the laws, uh . . . the morality, storm cellars, scientific discoveries and applications, insurance policies. So we subject our land and our seas to the . . . laws of balance sheets, the laws of mathematics, and forget the laws of Nature, the delicate exchange of ecosystems, the nurture of the soil, ya? Because it's all so primitive, hm?"

"You have nice eyes," she said.

"But Logos informed by the wisdom of Eros," he said, "that is another thing. Make me king of the world, Flora, and I would bring back Eros, saucy and big-bellied with life. There would be signboard adwertisements and television chingles."

Flora closed her eyes.

"Eros and Logos, the heart and the head in a cosmic

marriage. I like that," said the young man.

He said a great deal more but her attention drifted and returned, drifted and returned. All these new words. She'd never keep track of them. Ketzers and gene pools, and ecosystems and building a new planet with Eros and Logos coupling in the garden and a Green Party coalition in the next election and who gives a fat rat's ass.... I could never be married to this man, she thought, and fell asleep. When she awoke, the sun was low and red in the south and he was tugging at her to come and take a swim.

7.

Their last day by the river was hot. Lovemaking turned their bodies into water slides; they frolicked, slept, and lolled about all day long. In the late afternoon as the shadows of the trees lengthened and began to fall on the river, the young warden slept next to Flora on their blanket. He would be confined to the office after this, their seventh day together. They would have to tryst in Melville whenever he could drive over. Flora would be a teller again. She began to reassume some of her former severity. *I never did manage to figure out these deposit slips, dear. That's all right, Mrs. Finney, I'll fill it out again for you.*

Beside her, the young warden murmured, "I am der Ketzer."

Shortly after Whitey had left, Head Kreutzer showed up. The mosquitoes were bad, so she walked him up the path to Gopher Mountain, wondering if he suspected anything. He seemed oblivious, even when he sat on the knoll where all the grass had been flattened. "Nice view," he said.

The Ketzer

They wandered down from the knoll among the long shadows toward the poplars on the river bank. She was thinking it would be her last trip down here for a long time. At that moment she spotted the bear. It was sniffing Head's case of beer, the same scruffy old male she'd seen a week ago. She almost wanted to yell her salutations. The wind shifted and the bear became aware of them. It padded slowly into the saskatoon bushes and merged with the gloom of the thickets.

"I told you y'shoulda had a rifle," Head exclaimed.

"What for?" she said.

"You never know," he said.

"He's just showin you it's all right," she said.

"Those are his berries," he said.

"They're everyone's."

"I doubt if he's wild about sharin em."

"He's lettin us see that he lives here," she said. "He thinks you left him a gift."

"Yeah, great."

"He's got no reason to attack us. We're not chasin him. We're just walkin around."

Head went for his canoe, keeping a considerable amount of space between himself and where the bear had disappeared. Flora held her ground and lingered by the poplars. Head returned clutching a paddle. "You ask me," he said, "he was showin us the door."

"What are you doing with that?" she said.

"Come on," he said, nodding to the east. "I'll walk you up as far as the road."

FOUR

1.

Hunting with Steve and the guys felt wrong; she knew that now, but she couldn't turn back. It felt wrong as soon as she approached the lower meadow with Steve and saw the top of Gopher Mountain rising from the river like the head of a bald man. She could imagine what Whitey would say, or how the animals would clench inside as they approached, and she felt like a trespasser.

From the middle of the narrow meadow Neville beckoned wildly. "You want your chance, Harry?" he cried. He and the boys had spotted some fresh tracks in the new snow, a lot of them. Neville spoke with the excitement of a younger man. "You an Steve go halfway up on the left side of the bush. Spread out some. We got em corralled. Head an Clyde are up the other side and Goober's got the east end."

"Who's doggin?" Flora asked.

"I'm doggin," said Neville. "There's a big mother in that bush. Ain't nothin gettin by this time."

This time? Flora looked back at the bush in question, a long thin copse of willows and dogwood running down the centre of the meadow, only a few hundred yards from Flora's old hiding place. "This time" meant that Neville would spot the tracks in the fresh snow better than Clyde

The Ketzer

could ever have done. That other time. Goober's favourite story.

Steve took up a position about a hundred yards ahead of Flora. There was a draw between them where the water drained in the spring. Steve scanned the bush with the same sort of fervour she saw in all the men.

Neville never barked when he was the dog. Perhaps he assumed no one would ever mistake him for the thing he was hunting. But occasionally he swore, and Flora could hear this from time to time as he stumbled on a deadfall or took a willow branch in the face. He was moving fast.

There was a minute's silence and then he started to scream; it was like a plea: "Shoooot the buggers!"

All she could see was Steve, who looked back at her across the dip in the meadow. Then Steve yelled something and his gun went up. A doe leapt out of the bush and bounded into the draw between them, so close she could see an old scar on its shoulder. "It's a doe!" she cried, and Steve put up his gun.

The doe bounded down toward Gopher Mountain and the river. Out came Neville, spitting twigs, glaring at Flora. "Do you want some venison or dontcha?"

"That was a doe," she yelled back.

"Is history about to goddam repeat itself? Do you for chrissakes realize how long it'll be before we get another shot like that? *By* the *Jesus!*" He lurched back into the woods.

Steve and Flora shrugged at each other. Apparently the rules had changed. All around them the snow fell in heavier flakes, slanting into the hills in the late afternoon light. Steve turned his back to Flora, trying to see where the doe had gone. Once more her father swore and crashed into some deadwood. She wondered why this time he would swear first and crash second and another doe and a fawn bounded out. Once more they chose the draw between Steve and Flora as if it were some sort of safe passage. Steve was still gazing down toward the river. She cupped her hands to call to him. At that moment the buck emerged from the trees, silent, unmistakable. Appletree. The antlers were almost too massive for those of a white-tail. He seemed to be eyeing Steve, then jerked around to look at Flora. As Steve turned, the big buck began stiffly to trot their way.

Again came Neville's voice: "Shoot! Shoot! Shoot the bugger!"

The buck passed equidistant between Steve and Flora. The gun was at her shoulder, Appletree centred in her sights, and something red — Steve. He in her sights, she in his. Even at a hundred yards she caught his expression of absolute concentration.

"No!" she cried.

Neville crashed out of the bush.

Steve put up his gun, stumbled backward, and fell.

Neville fired and missed. The buck was too close for a scope. He tried to eject the shell. Again and again. "Harry, by all that's sacred!" he groaned.

The buck stopped to look at her. It seemed to sense something even before Flora threw the gun back up to her shoulder, and bounded down the draw toward Gopher Mountain.

Steve picked himself up from the snow, shook his hands.

Neville tore at his bolt.

The buck wheeled to the right suddenly and made for Flora's bush.

Flora fired.

2.

On their way back to the trucks they saw the moon come up, nearly full, with a copper blush. It lit their way through the narrow meadows. No one spoke.

Whenever he saw a slender shadow that somehow seemed separate from the surrounding trees, Neville wondered if it was a deer. Each time, he would clutch his rifle even harder (though not so the others could notice) and tense up his shoulders. He was tired. The hunt was over and he knew it, but he kept thinking, if I get half the chance, even if it's a night kill. . . .

The last illegal deer he dropped was a doe he and Clyde doubled on by the top road. They had field-dressed it on their own land in full view of a construction crew, and one of the men must have gotten right on the phone, because there was no love lost between Neville and those crews. They never seemed happy unless they were chewing up half the forest in the ranchland. The wardens got there before Neville or the boys could throw the doe into the truck. It had to be one of those bastards on construction. The guts were steaming and the snow was red, and the older of the two wardens dove in hands first. Neville, I'd swear this buck has no penis, he said. How do you figure that? Oh, I wouldn't know about them things, Neville said. I don't have no university degrees like you guys. Does this look like a penis to you, the older one says to the other, that whiteyhaired one. The younger one says, I got university degree, and where I come from those things are called waginas. You oughta know, says Clyde. Guys like

– 57 –

you pee sittin down, dontcha? The older one says, do you enjoy picking off does any time of the year, pregnant does like this one? And Neville says, do you enjoy takin orders from a frog in Ottawa?

"You look all in," Neville said at last to Flora.

She was picking her way along the trail ahead of Neville, stumbling, righting her stride, and carrying on. She shrugged at his observation. Likely she was brooding on how close she had come to nailing old Appletree. Change the subject, he thought. Change the goddam subject.

He wanted to tell Flora how he and Clyde had mouthed off to those wardens, how it was almost worth the fine and having their guns confiscated to see the look on their faces. He wanted to tell her, but he thought better of it. He'd probably told her often enough. Besides, any time he went on about the wardens, just to show him how independent she was — it was that perverse streak that ran so deep in Mernie — Flora would up and defend the wardens. Those bastards, he thought. They probably dined on venison that very night. It made him mad to think of it.

Neville's last legal deer was a four-point buck, only eighteen months old. And did he taste fine. Neville wanted to shout, It wasn't always this way, by the Jesus.

Before Flora came along, Neville and Head's father Harry Kreutzer could go out every fall with a team of horses and have two or three bucks or maybe an elk before dinner time. Neville and his friend Harry couldn't walk out to a haystack without seeing a dozen deer in broad daylight. When Neville was a boy he never knew a winter without deer sausage and mooseburger. They almost ran out of places to hang up the antlers.

The Ketzer

Flora had heard it all before.

They climbed out of the last meadow in single file and found the trail through the spruce groves that lead to the trucks. The moon had turned silver and cast diminishing blue shadows across the snow. Neville's rifle was on safety, but his arms, his entire torso, were cocked as though he expected the old days to come back again . . . before the goddam city hunters and their jeeps and those assholes from town runnin down fawns in their goddam snowmobiles and before the goddam wardens in their boy scout uniforms and their candy-ass government jobs takin orders from a goddam frog in Ottawa who wouldn't know a back hoe from a butter knife and all those goddam highway crews and railway crews shootin deer from a sidecar and those seismic bastards with their overland vehicles leavin gates open like they owned the place —

Flora stopped suddenly ahead of Neville. Everyone had stopped. In a clearing to Neville's right stood something the size of a sawhorse. A coyote? So be it. Neville snapped off his safety.

When he fired, the whole woods seemed to crack back. The animal went down on its back legs. They rushed the clearing as the creature tried to crawl into the spruce. It was a fawn of six months. The lower spine had been shattered, but still it struggled to reach the nearest clump of spruce trees.

All their scopes were fogged apparently. "Anyone got a knife?" Head said.

"Left mine in the truck," said Clyde.

"Every time I bring my skinnin knife," said Goober, "I end up never shootin nothin."

The fawn turned to look at them. It seemed to know that its mother was somewhere else and that this was the end, but it tried one last time to haul its body across the last bit of clearing. Game little chryster, Neville thought.

He called Flora over. "Our scopes don't work so close in, eh? How about you kill it?"

Flora moved forward into the half circle of men. "This is a fawn," she said.

"Yeah, well," Head mumbled.

"You couldn't make ten hotdogs outa this one," she said.

"Flora, just do it," said Goober.

She looked at them all.

The fawn began to bawl, and Flora seemed to be frozen to the spot. It was a curious childlike bleating, high and piercing. Neville wondered if these men had ever heard a fawn bawl before. He thought of his grandson and had a brief flash of his dream of the previous night.

Steve said, "Jesus."

"Kill it," said Neville. "Get it done with."

Head reached over for Flora's gun, gave her his own, cocked hers, raised it to his shoulder and fired. The fawn pitched forward into the snow.

As he gutted the fawn in the moonlight, Head brooded on Flora, how Mate had run out on her and how it was no wonder. She couldn't be one of the boys and she couldn't be one of the girls type thing, but she kept trying to be both. Isn't that just what Mate had said?

After a while Goober came over and held the flashlight for Head. Goober tried to think of one thing he might say

The Ketzer

to Flora. The first thing that came to his mind was, Too bad about just nickin Appletree, Harry. But he thought better of it. Maybe something like, C'mon Harry, the boys are waitin. Let's go get pissed. Something like that.

Clyde broke out the beer and offered it around. "Victory drink, eh? First one ta-night."

Neville pissed in the snow and drank his beer at the same time, a sad fatigue carved by the moon on the lines of his face. I don't give a good goddam, he thought fervently. Harry gets the sausage from this one.

"I've been wondering what it must feel like to haul a rifle around when your heart's not in it," Steve said to Flora. She shrugged. He sat beside her in Goober's half-ton waiting to see her lean forward so the moon would illuminate the side of her face. A few hours earlier he had decided to tell her his philosophy of hunting, that the real hunter loves the thing he kills. Somehow that seemed a bit beside the point. He thought and thought about what he might say to her to redeem the moment. He felt a soft "plop" in his lap.

"Here's your gloves back," she said.

Later, when Head had washed up in the snow, he sat next to Flora in the truck where Steve had sat. They were all about ready to move out. He said, "You done okay out there, Harry."

Without turning in the seat, she said, "Well, if I done okay out there, I guess you and the boys must of done fabulous."

3.

When Steve awoke, the fires were faded, the sun up, and there were voices outside. One of them was Head's. Steve rolled out of his bag and peered through the kitchen window. Head was talking to a man in a yellow jeep. He was handsome, stocky, wore his hair long, and wore shades. He wondered it he'd seen him at the Ski Shack. He looked familiar.

Head was clutching a large wad of twenties. He seemed torn between the need to pocket the money and the need to count it. "Yeah, well," he said to the fellow in the shades. Their conversation, apparently, was over.

Steve yawned. He felt only half rested. He'd been dogged by bad dreams all night long. At first it was obscure creatures chasing him through the woods. Then it was a weird spectacle down at Neville's corral. A bunch of guys gathered to watch the rooster with no head. Taking bets.

Head came in. "You're up!" he shouted. "Jee-zus."

"What was that all about?" said Steve.

"That's for me to know an you to find out. Hey, are we goin huntin or what?"

Steve dressed for his last morning in the woods. He would take it easy today. He hoped that Neville and the boys would be too busy on the ranch to hunt. He also hoped he could see Flora one more time. But briefly. Because then it would be just him and Head, two guys with one thought: get a buck and get out.

Head threw Steve's .308 up to his shoulder and swung it at the bear hide on the wall.

"Can you tell me one thing?" said Steve.

– 62 –

The Ketzer

"Pow."

"Seriously."

"It'll cost ya."

"That rooster over at Potts's. Once he got his head chopped off, could he still make out with the hens?"

Head laughed. "How the hell would I know?"

"Seriously."

"Mernie didn't seem to think so."

Steve told him part of his dream, that the men were betting on whether the rooster could cover a hen within a specified time limit.

Head only stopped laughing when the bacon started to smoke. "I'm sharin the cabin with a certified loony," he said.

"Hey," Steve said, "what was goin down out there?"

"Sell me your Winchester scope an all, I'll tell ya anything. I'll even not bullshit ya." Head wore a mischievous look.

"Who was that guy in the jeep? I keep thinking I've seen him somewhere."

Head regarded Steve out of the corner of his eye, crammed a piece of toast into his mouth, washed it down with instant coffee, and said, "You seen him once last August or so in the weight room with me."

"Of course."

"That was Mate."

They packed up the truck so that Head could lock the cabin. While Head was outside, Steve took a quick look into the utility room. The tarp was thrown into the corner and all the antlers were gone.

"Well, Neville," Head declared, stretching his long arms, "if you folks are workin today, me an Steve'll hit the lower meadow again. That okay by you?"

"Give er hell," said Neville.

Flora came into the kitchen carrying her baby. She moved past the men and spoke in hushed tones to her mother. Steve vowed that before the day was over he would make her laugh.

She turned to look at Steve. There seemed to be a purpose in her staring, but no visible emotion. Her gaze reminded Steve of a way some animals have of looking at people. She brought Carrie over and said, "Would you hold him?"

Steve grunted in reply, reddening.

"Last night you was wonderin what's it like to hold a rifle when your heart's not in it," she said. "Well, here's my answer." She handed him the baby. "Don't worry, his cold's almost gone. And he's shot his wad this morning, so he ain't even loaded."

Mernie laughed, Neville smiled, but Flora remained impassive and joined her mother where the pantry joined the kitchen. They were doing pies together.

Steve held the baby as though it were an expensive urn. Head settled back down into his chair, brooding at Flora's backside. Neville left at Goober's bidding. The kettle rocked and snored on the stove.

Steve discovered Flora's baby regarding him with what seemed to be a look of appraisal. There was something extraterrestrial about the face, the elf-like ears, the precocious mop of whitey blond hair, the unusually well-defined nose, the adult look in those pale blue eyes, the dispassionate inspection the baby seemed to be giving him. We have landed and we are being held by a hoser from the

The Ketzer

city. We may have to bail out on this one. Over.

"Are we huntin or what?" Head finally asked.

Steve looked Flora's way. She was spooning saskatoon berries into one of Mernie's pie shells. She licked the spoon and a listlessness like a cloud seemed to drift over her face. Sometimes Cora got that look.

But Cora was different. She wasn't so. . . . Various terms for female malaise presented themselves to Steve: screwed up, unreadable, bitchy, hot and cold. None of them seemed to work. Ornery? Contrary?

"Time to hit the road," said Head, putting his mug down and rising.

"Maybe yiz can get a grown-up one this time," said Flora.

"Maybe you should join up with them wardens," Head replied.

"It takes more guts t'hunt down a buncha game hogs than it does t'shoot a fawn." She glared first at Head, then at Steve.

"Don't look at me," Steve said.

Carrie began to bawl. For a moment Steve had forgotten the baby was on his lap. His pale face was now red and contorted. "Jeez," he said to Flora, "I think I scared the kid."

4.

Steve and Head made it all the way down to the lower meadow before they found the tracks of Appletree. They led from Flora's bush back out to the lower meadow and meandered from browse to browse. This had Head buffaloed.

"He's not runnin, he's *feedin* for God's sake. Look where he lifts his foot. He's goin slow as hell."

"So?"

"Well, Schuyler, it's obvious. He's not runnin from anythin, he's feedin. Look, if you had six hunters on your tail last night an just got nicked by a bullet, would you stop for some horse duvers?"

Steve gazed at the hills where the buck's trail wandered.

Head continued, "Harry said that Appletree must of got past us in the dark. After she nicked him an we had him surrounded. Remember? When she was in there doggin," he said, pointing to Flora's bush, "an we was all on point. Are you with me?"

Steve nodded.

Head went on. "We had him surrounded an Harry says, 'He's gone.' Remember?"

"Yeah."

Head asked, "What did she say to you?"

Steve thought a moment. "She said Appletree must have been going like sixty. It was too dark to see him escape."

"Right. He was goin like sixty. But none of us *seen* him goin like sixty an there's no runnin tracks." Head retraced the path of the big buck on the meadow. "Steve, he was goddam *walkin* outa the bush. *Browsin*. There's no other tracks."

Steve pointed to Flora's bush, from which the tracks had emerged. "Let me check the thicket," he said. Steve liked solving mysteries.

He waded into the thicket where Flora had walked the previous night immediately after firing at Appletree. He followed in her footsteps. The sun was high and bright, and Steve could even see the bluish trails of mice and chickadees in the snow. Here and there among Flora's tracks were the splayfooted tracks of Appletree. At various points

The Ketzer

along the trail their tracks came together and made a single path in the snow. He followed her trail into the middle of the thicket until their footsteps circled a little marsh, and still there was only one path, as though Flora and Appletree had been taking a walk together.

Steve waded silently through the snow. He did not want to give away his position. Just in case.

An odd feeling came over him, as though Flora were here in the bush, watching him, eyeing the way he held his gun.

In his dream the previous night he'd held a revolver, his old cap gun from when he'd lived on Moxon Crescent, and the headless rooster was just beginning to feather one of the hens when Flora showed up, naked, for all the men to see. But instead of putting on a show for the guys at the corral as they clapped and whistled, she seemed to be in a state of wild distress. She looked right at Steve and said something to him, she looked him right in the eye, it was an urgent look.

He stumbled on something and had to catch his balance. It was a huge antler.

"Kreutzer!" he yelled. "You're not gonna believe this!"

Head yelled back, "Is he dead?"

"No. Hang on," Steve called, glad to hear his friend's voice close by.

He circled the little frozen marsh to the left. He followed the same trail around to where he had begun, to the place where the buck had left Flora's path and wandered out into the meadow to feed. Near this place, where the willows and grass were thickest, the buck had apparently bedded down for the night, right on the path. So he must have remained in this thicket until well after Flora and the hunters had gone home.

Steve did the circuit again. It was a flower-shaped path. In one place Flora had broken trail on her own. This side trip had taken her to the centre of the little pond where she had apparently stopped to pee.

And from this vantage point, from the ovule of the flower, so to speak, she could have seen — Steve did a complete circle, his eyes like the lenses of a film camera; he saw aspens, cattails, rosebushes, willows — she could have seen everything.

"She must have seen him," he told Head.

Head was inspecting the big antler.

Steve said, "I mean after she took that potshot. She went in there and saw him."

Head squinted at Steve, his mouth open.

Steve said, "Weird, eh?"

5.

Flora remembered she had fired because Neville had told her afterward. She remembered Neville pleading, *Harry, by all that's sacred*! and Steve slipping, and a jolt somewhere inside of her body (like one of those old-fashioned flashpowder photographs in black and white) that made her different after, frozen in time and somehow broken (she would never manage to explain how or why), and a whiff of gunpowder: the great buck seemed to stumble, lurch, and toss his head, then gather for another leap. Up he went, bounding like a jack rabbit, and never stopping until he was swallowed up by the thicket. And there he must have waited.

The Ketzer

Something else had happened, something broken off and lost between the flashpowder jolt and the buck's wild dance, and this too she tried to reassemble, staring at the falling snow and the edge of the woods.

She found herself walking toward the trees. Neville strode past her, red and puffing, eyes to the ground, his big nose snuffling. "You nicked him, Harry," he babbled. "I seen it."

They hurried to the edge of the woods and peered through the trees. Neville found the trail but no blood. He yelled to Steve, "Goober an Head went around. They're waitin on the other side. We got im trapped!" Neville barked out his orders to Steve like an officer: "If he goes left an runs for the ridge, you take him. If he goes this way, he's mine."

The two men walked in opposite directions along the fringe of the bush, waiting for the big buck to plunge out, but he stayed and they couldn't spot him. Flora walked behind her father, lost, like a girl in a dream, the falling snow like dream snow, her father a dark shape like the father long ago who would come in from the hallway to tuck her in at night and she pretending to be asleep. Wave after wave of dissonant sounds. She kept thinking about the buck, remembering the words of the warden's assistant, *The whole problem with man is with the head*, seeing once more the head of the buck on the bead of her gun barrel.

She stumbled on something and picked it up, an antler at the edge of the bush, a huge one, cracked and shattered near the base. *Oh please, God, please.*

"Harry!"

Neville's voice seemed to come from very far away, and in the fading light he was even more like a figure in a dream.

– 69 –

"You go in for him, Harry. We'll pick him off if he makes a break for it."

She picked up his trail and moved slowly through the bush, her bush, unfamiliar now because it was almost dark and almost winter. She was shaking. She went slow as a porcupine. She found the tracks easily but no blood.

Forgetting to bark, she moved as though in a dream, lurching over the thornbushes and deadwood, deeper into the heart of the thicket. In the centre was her little frozen pond perhaps thirty feet across. The buck had gone toward it. Instead of heading out the other side of the bush toward Goober or Head or Clyde, the tracks veered left and circled the pond. She followed and they doubled back toward the meadow. *Oh please, dear God*. She could hear the voices of her father and Steve not a hundred feet away, so she wondered what would possess the big animal that he would head toward the men instead of away from them. But a few yards from the edge of the bush, the tracks went left again, back into the thicket. She stumbled along in his trail, peering through the fading light, tired now, having to urinate, hearing the men call her name. They expected something from her. She wouldn't answer though, or the buck would hear her. Back around the little marsh she went and realized the buck had chosen the same trail.

She stopped. If she was following him, then he was following her. They could go on walking the same circle till after dark. She looked behind her and to her left across the little pond. There was still only one broken trail, his and hers. (It was right by that clump of willows she had touched the moose calf, while across the pond, the cow had munched on lilies. She had touched the calf on the flank

The Ketzer

and it scarcely acknowledged her presence, the surest guarantee of her invisibility that she could hope for. Then the calf joined the cow and they both looked her way.)

She felt a steady pain along her arm and realized that all this time she'd been carrying the antler. She dropped it on the trail. It felt as though she were leaving a note for Appletree. She carried on. Again she heard her name called but she had made up her mind not to bark. She went around the little pond once more to be sure he hadn't left the circle they both had made. But he stayed on the track and again circled back toward her father, and around again just before the edge of the bush. She came upon the antler and her heart sank. She'd been expecting to see him this time. It was almost as if he hadn't received her message, or didn't trust it. She peered through the woods. The dark was falling. There was time, perhaps, for one more trip around the circuit. She stayed on the path and began once again to circle the little marsh, and a semicircle away from the antler, she stopped, looked around, and waited until she could feel the cold settling into her bones, saw nothing, heard only the occasional call from one of the men. Then she stepped inside the circle, onto the ice, and headed across toward the antler. In the centre of the pond she stopped and looked about, took down her jeans and urinated in the snow. When she stood up again she sensed something behind her, something like the bear in summer. Slowly she turned around. The big buck stood on the trail by the marsh, head low, watching her. In the dim light she could still make out his one remaining antler like the branches on her mother's apple tree.

"I'm sorry," she said.

FIVE

1.

Flora deposited Carrie on the sofa, drew up the blind, and opened a window in the tiny living room. The late autumn air seemed to follow the sun into the room. The snow had almost melted.

"Bok!" cried the baby. His cold seemed to have vanished.

Outside on the street Steve was leaning against the Toyota truck while Head checked their gear in the back. Already Head was sulking, back in harness, beginning to see toilets and sewer pipes, or so it appeared to Flora. *Know what I do t'get ridda the stink?*

"Bok!" cried the baby again.

She picked him up, exposing his face to the sun and looked at him. "Are you my fella?" she said.

The baby smiled.

"Bok," was the answer, and she laughed.

"Come see," she said, and carried him over to an arched recess in the living room wall where she kept the phone. Out of sight behind the phone was a polaroid shot of a man's face. He wore a foolishly happy smile. Flora showed the baby this photo. "See Daddy," she said.

"Bok," said the baby.

Flora laughed again and returned to the window. Still

- 72 -

laughing, she looked out the window and caught Steve and Head looking in at her from the truck, as though she were.... It took her a moment to figure it out. Never seen someone laugh before, she wanted to shout, but squinted back and tried to imagine both of them with rifles raised, aiming. Yes, that was the expression they wore.

2.

In Toronto it was a bit before midnight. Cora would be in her nighty but not yet asleep. Unshowered, tired, and half-undressed, Steve dialled her number. He sat on his mattress on the floor, fingering some unopened mail on his pillow. He was depressed.

"You asleep?" he began.

His voice was hushed, as though someone were listening, and he smiled nervously into the mouthpiece. "I would've but where I was this weekend there weren't any phones.... Out hunting.... The Assiniboine Valley, away east of here, way out in the boonies. We had this neat cabin. Guy named Kreutzer, real nice guy.... Yeah.... Yeah.... I wondered how those got there. You put them there last June? ... Of course I still have them.... Yes, they kept my hands nice and warm...."

They spoke for some time, Steve's voice modulating from taciturnity ("It's no big deal, y' know") to a gentle chiding tone that, for Steve ("You always worry about that, you shouldn't worry about that"), was unfamiliar territory.

Then later, "Of course we should be seeing each other at Christmas, of course I'm coming down there! What are you saying?" he cried, his face suddenly stricken like a child's. "Where is all this coming from?"

He looked out over the mess he had made of his apartment, his gym socks and sweats tossed in a heap on the sofa, a case of empties and spilled Cheezies on the matching chair, his rifle and hunting clothes sprawled like a dead soldier on the bedroom floor.

"I phoned you because I missed you, because I was feeling . . . you know. . . . I phoned you because I thought you'd be wondering. . . . What are you saying? This doesn't sound like you. . . . I don't have my reservation yet, no, but that's just a formality. I'm *coming* to Toronto. . . . I *phoned* because, because I thought it was time we stopped kidding ourselves, it's time to cut the crap. . . . "

He listened with his head on his hand then held the phone at arm's length, his other hand reaching out as if to feel for rain, his eyes rolled toward Heaven, then resumed his huddled pose and listened as she spoke.

"Just let me ask you one thing. . . . Never mind that. . . . Cora! . . . Well, you make it sound like we're just goddam penpals. . . . Well, of *course* it bothers me!"

Later, after the late news on TV and the weekend review of sports, and a couple of beers, and much pacing, after he'd made up his mind that *he* would not be the one to call back first, Steve opened his mail. The last piece was a small parcel with no return address. It was wrapped in brown paper (an old grocery bag?) and tied with old string. There was a note and something light in a small plastic bag. He opened the plastic bag before reading the note because the thing in the bag smelled funny.

"Jesus!" he barked. It was the head of a chicken, long dead. The note read as follows:

The Ketzer

Dear Mr. Schuyler

Inclosed is a trophy head for the wall of your apartment. Our club members felt this head would be more use to you than to its original owner. When you do the mesurments, you will note that this head realy ranks up thier with the national trophys for chickens over the last decade or more, this head intitles you to a lifetime membership in the Kreutzer Hunting Lodge so when this here chicken starts to talk to you you lissen. But when you start to talk back, you know its time to come hunting again come out here P.D.Q. where the hunting is fine. Bring this here head with you and show it at the door then we will know you are one of us.

Your sincerely,

H. Kreutzer
President

Steve was in no mood for a joke, but as he read and reread the letter, a sardonic half-smile came to his lips. Before showering, he wrapped the chicken head in the note and placed them back in the little plastic bag. Then he put the little package in the freezing compartment of his fridge because he didn't want to stink things up.

That night he dreamt once more he was being pursued in an apple orchard by men with guns but this time he couldn't find his cap pistol. One of his pursuers had a grin like Head Kreutzer. They drove him out of the orchard and he fled through space. His cries were heard across the galaxy. Even Cora heard him, every time she picked up the telephone.

3.

At an altitude of approximately 36,000 kilometres, a number of synchronous satellites orbit our planet. They are called synchronous because they stay in one position over the earth, and their motion is synchronized with its spin. During the time it takes for Earth to rotate once on its axis, the satellites also complete one orbit; like Zeno's Achilles or lovers on an urn, they are embarked upon an endless pursuit.

One particular satellite, looking somewhat like a huge bottlecap with attached brush (the kind one finds on a bottle of white correction fluid or certain brands of nail polish), floats above the mid-Atlantic in a cold infinity of stars. It has been seen as a speck of grit in the Big Dipper and a fourth stud on Orion's belt. Yet one is mostly struck by its forlorn disconnection from everything else in the universe; everything, that is, except its apparent loyalty to a specific swatch of spinning sea.

A discarded remnant, perhaps, of some passing intelligence? An icon from some religion whose prayer books have been burned, theologians buried, tablets long since ground to dust? A piece broken off a larger machine? In fact, it is potentially all of these things; it is a communications satellite linking two ground stations, both with powerful antennae that rise like antlers in the night. One of these stations is near Boise, Idaho, the other in Goonhilly Downs, England.

The Ketzer

Perched upon this satellite with a specially tuned listening device, we could hear the many signals coming in via Boise, one wavering through space from Melville, Saskatchewan: "I thought I'd show Dad I could drop a buck; I mean those guys think I'm useless as balls on the Pope, and damn it, they had to see. . . ." and another signal, via the Downs, coming in from Hamburg: "You mean you have tried to bring down this great creature, this Appletree, on purpose?" Back and forth the signals go as our satellite follows the globe rolling like a gutter ball through the universe. "You get caught up sometimes. In someone else's thing?" "Ya." "An you figure, what the hell, go with it." The voices seem to lose their connection, so verbally they grope for each other in the dark until the signals become stronger, the right words spoken again. "Bless you, Flora." "I seen him again and didn't say Boo, I just walked out an told the guys he'd taken off, an they believed me!" ". . . der Ketzer." Interference. Thunder somewhere over the Downs. "What?" "Ketzer. The one who defies orders . . . holy orders . . . the technocratic imperative. . . . *Bruderlichkeit*, ya?" "What? Yeah, anyway, those buggers, they couldn't nail a buck so they went an shot a fawn about the size of our dogs. I'm tellin you, Whitey, I've had it with huntin." "My God. . . ." Pause. Static. "You still there, Whitey?" "Vitey. I love that name." "I got his antler. The guys, they give it to me." "Flora, I must go to work. Next time. . . ." Pause, crackle. ". . . reverse charges, ya?" "Ya, Whitey." "I love that name."

4.

Another kind of signal, drifting from the hocks of a doe in oestrus, carried by the night wind across the meadow and floating through a grassy thicket, brings up the head of the greatest buck in the valley. His single antler weighs like the memory of a bad fall, but he struggles out of his grassy pallet stiffly to his feet.

The doe stands several hundred yards away in the centre of the meadow. She is the one with the old scar on her shoulder. She has stopped feeding on the alfalfa to listen. Something unfurling inside her is blowing musk to the November wind and her tail twitches back and forth.

The Ketzer is set in ITC Galliard, a Mannerist revival typeface designed by Matthew Carter, based on the designs of the sixteenth-century French master Robert Granjon. It was issued by Linotype in 1978 and later licensed by the International Typeface Corporation. Chapter and subsection headings are set in Galliard Black.

This book was designed and typeset by Donald Ward.